MW00944565

#2
Texas State Park Adventures

The Palo Duro Lighthouse Race

by Jefferson Marshall
illustrated by Shawn Taylor

COTTONWOOD
PUBLISHING

Texas State Park Adventures #2:
The Palo Duro Lighthouse Race
Published by Cottonwood Publishing
302 E. Highway 62, No. 798
Wolfforth, Texas 79382
texasstateparkadventures.com

Printed in the United States of America.

ISBN: 978-1-7334606-1-3

For Tony Peterman and TBM LTC
"As iron sharpens iron"

CONTENTS

We were explorers on the verge of something

big, and every great journey entails hardship.

Tommy Caldwell

The Push

1
FIELD TRIP

I felt free now with the bus window down. A breeze met me as I looked out. I was glad to be on a field trip and away from school. The wheels on the bus spun round as my gaze rested on the open countryside passing by. I smiled in the light of the warm sun.

A road sign read "TX-217". The bus passed a lonely house with chipping paint, surrounded by interesting, rusted farming equipment. A small windmill spun in the far distance, reflecting bits of the sun off its rotating blades.

There was an old cemetery surrounded by a thin, black fence. I held my breath and belly button as we passed. My older brothers had warned me about ghosts, so I wasn't taking any chances.

I was seated next to the window, sharing the row with Kenrick and Ivan. The grey back of the seat in front of us had designs in it, probably carved with a small knife or paperclip.

Kenrick and Ivan traced over the designs with their fingers as they argued about video games. Ivan had beaten a level first and

Kenrick was jealous. I was jealous of both of them because my video game console was ancient.

I tried to keep up with their conversation, but my mind was elsewhere. It was hard to sit still, my thoughts were caught up in a whirlwind of excitement as I looked out the window again.

I hoped to have a great adventure. I hoped this place would be amazing.

Ms. Donner stood up at the front of the yellow dog bus to speak.

"Good work on your projects in class," said Ms. Donner. "Each of you have learned quite a bit about the history, science, literature, and even math of this region. You have earned this field trip with your hard work.

We're grateful to our parent volunteers with us as well, who've helped to make this trip possible.

To celebrate what you have learned, we are taking you camping for the next couple of days to Palo Duro Canyon. However, be prepared. You will also be facing a challenge before the trip is over."

"A challenge! What kind of challenge?" a couple students asked.

"I can't say anything more for now," said Ms. Donner "but sit tight and we will tell you more tonight. That rhymed!" She chuckled as she sat down.

"What do you think will be the challenge?" Kenrick asked Ivan and me as we pressed our feet up against the seats in front of us.

"I don't know," I said, "but do you think we'll get to have partners?"

"I bet the three of us would win if we were on the same team," Kenrick said.

"Yeah," said Ivan. "It's not like anyone else here could beat us."

"Do you guys remember surviving Caprock Canyons?" I asked.

"We remember Caprock Canyons," smiled Mari, turning around from the seat in front of us, "and stop kicking the back of my chair, Ivan."

"Make me, Mari." Ivan kicked the back of the chair harder just to annoy his little sister.

"That's it!" yelled Mari. "I don't care what the competition is, Ashley and I are going to win it because you won't stop kicking my chair!"

"Yeah!" shouted Ashley, sitting next to Mari.

"I reckon y'all are mistaken," I joked. "Nice Rangers hat by the way, Mari!"

"Thanks Colter. I like your hat too," smiled Mari quickly "but there's no way we would lose in a competition to you three. That's just silly."

"You're silly," I said, sticking my tongue out.

"Well anything you guys can do, we can do better" sneered Mari.

"No. We can do anything better than you," Ivan shot back.

"No, you can't," glared Ashley at Ivan.

"Oh, yes we can," Kenrick chuckled, sticking his tongue out too.

"Ms. Donner! Colter is sticking his tongue out at me!" Mari yelled; her hand raised in the air.

"You two, please quit scuffling back there or I will have to assign seats for the whole bus," said Ms. Donner firmly.

"Yes ma'am," we shouted.

"Hey, I think we're here!" said Kenrick, sliding the window down and looking out. "I think we finally made it!"

2
LOOKOUT POINT

Buses crept through the line of cars waiting to enter the park. Heads poked out of the bus for glimpses of the canyon.

A huge, wooden sign read "Palo Duro Canyon State Park" in white letters.

Making it through the gate, we saw a small herd of Texas long-horned cattle.

They were grazing on a giant, round bale of hay. A calf stretched over the edge of the water trough, barely tall enough to get a sip of the cool water in the tank.

"How adorable," squealed Ashley "they're just like the cattle at my dad's house, except with a lot longer horns, that's for sure."

"You have cattle?" Ivan asked, interested.

"My dad does, he breeds Black Angus," said Ashley "and he has a few horses."

"You aren't scared of cows?" I asked.

"Of course not," Ashley said shocked, "they're more afraid of you than you are of them."

"Place your bottoms on the seat while the bus is still moving," said Ms. Donner.

We sat back down in our seats, still peering out the windows as the bus made its way slowly down the road leading from the canyon rim into the park.

"Wow, look over there," I said, catching my first glimpse of the drop off into the canyon.

Everyone rose to look out the window again.

"Place your bottoms on the seat while the bus is still moving," said Ms. Donner a second time.

We sat back down again, anxious to see more of the canyon.

"How far do you think the drop off is?" asked Kenrick.

"I bet it's one thousand feet to the bottom," said Ashley.

"Why are we stopping already?" asked Mari, as the bus pulled into a parking lot.

"Okay everyone," said Mr. Alvarez, "you may hop out at this lookout point before we head down into the canyon."

"Sweet!" Kenrick shouted, hopping into the center aisle to jump off the bus.

As we piled out of the yellow dog, we made our way to a short rock wall on the edge of the canyon.

"Wow, look how massive the canyon is," hollered Mari, keeping a safe distance from the edge.

"It's so cool," I said, leaning over the rock wall to see better, "look how far the canyon goes!"

I gazed out as far as I could, looking over the many formations of the canyon and down onto the trails winding through the park. There was too much to take in all at once and so much to see.

"Look at how small everything looks from up here," said Mari.

"Yeah, those hikers down there look like tiny little ants," pointed Kenrick.

"I wonder what kinds of animals live down there?" asked Ashley.

"I wonder where the snack bar is," joked Ivan, looking through a pair of binoculars.

"Where did you get those binoculars?" I asked Ivan, surprised.

"Well what are we doing standing around here chit-chatting," yelled Kenrick. "Let's get down into the canyon!"

We ran and hopped back onto the bus.

The bus weaved its way down the canyon, taking slow turns and pumping the breaks often.

The yellow dog lurched its way down a steep, curvy road that was the final stretch into the canyon.

Everyone held on tight as gravity pushed us into the seat cushion in front of us.

The side of the canyon had different-colored layers of rock. We were told each layer was formed during different time periods of the earth.

The canyon walls were painted red, tan, orange, and white, with a thin layer of yellow rock too.

I think Ms. Donner said the white, shiny rock was called Gypsum.

We kept making our way through the park.

We drove around sharp corners, and over bridges with streams of red, muddy water flowing underneath.

Soon, we arrived at our camping spot called "Hackberry Camping Area."

3
POTATO CHIPS

We grabbed our bags, sleeping stuff, and tents from underneath the bus seats. Everyone tried to push and shove their way to the sliding exit door.

"One at a time please," shouted Ms. Donner "single-file line."

We pushed and shoved until we reached the light of day outside of the school bus.

Everyone carried a hodge-podge of camping supplies, borrowed tents or sleeping bags, and clothes jammed into backpacks.

Ivan carried his clothes in a military duffle that he borrowed from his dad. My clothes were in a blue hand-me-down duffle bag with the strap about to fall off. Ashley had a small suitcase, and Mari and Kenrick both carried cotton string bags.

Hackberry Camp Area looked like it was straight out of a Wild West movie. The landscape was dry with rocks, red dirt, and little grass.

"Now listen up, everyone," shouted Mr. Alvarez through his megaphone, "ladies' tents will be in these spots to the left and gentlemen's tents will be to the right."

He pointed as he told us which directions to set up camp.

"We've practiced setting up tents in gym class, so now it's your turn to show what you've learned! Be sure to help each other out." Mr. Alvarez continued, "we'll meet together again in thirty minutes to go over our schedule for the next few days."

Kenrick and I decided to tent together. Ivan decided to share a tent with another school friend of ours named Max.

"Hi, Max," Kenrick and I said.

"Hey guys," Max replied. "Where do you plan to set up your tent?"

"We haven't decided yet," said Kenrick.

"You can set up next to Ivan and me if you want," suggested Max. "It's nice and flat over here, plus it's super grassy."

"Sounds great," I smiled.

Kenrick picked a red two-person tent because red is his favorite color. He opened the tent bag, letting the tent, stakes, poles, and rainfly fall out onto the ground.

We rolled out the tent, unfolding it and flapping it in the breeze like a parachute.

"The tent sounds weird when you wave it in the wind," laughed Kenrick, "like a crunchy bag of potato chips."

"Thanks, Kenrick," I snickered. "Now I'm hungry for potato chips."

We kept unraveling the tent until it was completely spread out on the ground.

"Wavy potato chips," I said, my mouth watering.

We grabbed the tent poles, piecing the sections together into two long poles.

"Crunchy potato chips," Kenrick laughed.

We slid the poles through their sheaths.

"Salty potato chips," I sighed longingly.

"Cheesy potato chips," Kenrick said, winking.

"Cheesy potato chips?" I asked, confused.

"Yeah," said Kenrick, "the ones sprinkled with cheese dust that leave your fingers all orangey.

The kind you have to get the cheese dust off by licking your fingers clean or else you'll get the dust all over your shirt and your parents get mad at you for ruining your new clothes."

"Oh, that kind of potato chip," I laughed.

We placed one side of the pole into the corner grommet. When we placed the other side of the first pole into the opposite grommet, it made the pole curve into a bow shape.

"One more pole to go," I said.

"Sweet," Kenrick replied, "easy-peasy."

We got one end of the second pole into the grommet, but the other end was tricky because the tent kept moving.

"I can't get it," I said. "It won't stop moving around. What do we do?"

I looked over at Ivan and Max. They were already finished setting up their tent and were relaxing inside with the front flap open. Ivan was munching down on a chocolate bar.

"Let's ask Ivan and Max for help," Kenrick suggested. "Hey guys, do you mind helping us get this last tent pole in?"

"Why would we help you two?" Ivan smirked, taking another bit of chocolate. "Just kidding. We'll help you." Ivan sat down his chocolate bar, closing up the wrapper and putting on top of his pillow.

"Thanks guys," I said.

"You're welcome," said Max.

"What's your favorite kind of chips?" I asked Max.

"Um...," thought Max. "Sea salt and vinegar."

"Ew, gross," said Ivan, sticking his tongue out.

With Max and Ivan's help, we got the poles put in. Then they returned to their tent.

The tent stakes were tough to hammer because the ground was pretty hard. We took turns using a rubber mallet to hammer the stakes into the ground.

"Should we put the rainfly on?" Kenrick asked.

"I guess," I sighed, thinking a rainfly was silly.

"Lame. I don't think we'll need it," laughed Kenrick, helping me put the rainfly on top.

"Should we roll out our sleeping bag and set our stuff out right now?"

"Nah," said Kenrick. "I don't want to. Let's do that tonight."

Kenrick threw his gear into the middle of the tent floor.

"Sounds great to me," I smiled, chunking all my camping stuff into the same pile. "It looks like we're done."

"Hey, Ivan?" Kenrick asked. "Do you have any more chocolate bars? That looks delicious."

4
WELCOME TO PALO DURO

"Attention everyone," said Mr. Alvarez over the megaphone, "the State Park Rangers of Palo Duro are here to speak with us."

"Good afternoon, ladies and gentlemen. I'm Interpretive Ranger Stacey" she began. "Welcome to Palo Duro Canyon State Park.

My job is to show you around the park, tell you about the history and geology of the park, and answer any questions you have along the way.

Palo Duro has been home to many wonderful groups of people: Folsom, Apache, Spaniards, and ranchers.

In the 1930's, a group of young men, known as the Civilian Conservation Corps, helped turn Palo Duro into a state park for many to enjoy. The C.C.C. added roads and buildings, including our park visitor's center. This park has many trails, interesting caves, and unique rock formations.

Another spectacular attraction is a musical drama put on in the park every summer. It begins with a man on horseback carrying the Texas flag proudly while his horse gallops along the cliff of the canyon wall.

Over the next couple days, you and your friends will be roughing it outside and competing in a challenge, so my fellow state park ranger, Ranger Mendez, thought it might be fun to teach you how to safely start a fire. You'll want to pay close attention, this information may be important for you to use later in our challenge."

We leaned in closer as she mentioned the word "fire."

"Hello Everyone. I'm Ranger Mendez. Thanks to all the rain we've had lately, our recent fire ban has been lifted, so it's a perfect time to learn how to start a fire." Ranger Mendez bent down and began to pick up sticks. "Before starting your fire, you need to gather your materials. Does anyone know the rule about collecting firewood in a state park?"

Mari's hand shot up. "I do! You can't gather wood in a state park because we want to leave everything better than the way we found it."

"You're absolutely correct," said Ranger Mendez. "You are not allowed to collect any firewood within a state park. Today, we are providing your groups firewood of different sizes.

First, you'll need what's called 'kindling.' Kindling is very tiny pieces of wood, smaller than a matchstick.

Second, you'll need 'tinder.' It's wood ranging from pencil to quarter size in diameter.

Lastly, you need to use 'fuel.' That's the larger material like logs, but we won't be needing those today for our fires.

You will only be needing 'kindling' and 'tinder.'"

State Park Ranger Mendez sat down in the dirt next to the campfire pit. Our school group gathered around him to watch. I peered over Kenrick's shoulder to see Ranger Mendez's demonstration better.

He placed two large sticks in a V-shape on the ground, then placed one stick resting across the first two so it would be raised off the ground. Gently, he stacked a thin row of kindling (the really, really small twigs) across the stick that was off the ground, creating a little lean-to of sticks.

"Ranger Mendez?" Max asked, raising his hand "can't you just pour gasoline or oil on the wood to start a fire?"

"Good question," said Ranger Mendez "if you use gasoline, the fumes will ignite and you'll have an explosion. That would be bad."

"Whoa," said Kenrick, smiling.

"If you use oil," Ranger Mendez continued "your fire will burn until the oil or grease runs out. It's very dangerous.

I would recommend using a small amount of lighter fluid if you want extra fuel, but my favorite is to just use a match and materials that nature provides."

After answering Max's question, Ranger Mendez laid down on his stomach. He was right beside his pile of sticks.

He struck a match on the side of a matchbox and cradled the flame with his hand to protect it from the wind. He quickly placed the small match flame under the kindling.

The flame caught ever so slightly.

He moved the match around the pile to catch the kindling in a few more spots before tossing it on top of the twigs.

Slowly, he added more tiny sticks, then slightly larger ones to make the flame grow higher.

He blew on the flame gently to spark it back to life whenever the flame grew dim or was close to going out. The fire began to grow and crackle loudly. "Excellent," said Ranger Mendez "Now let's test your fire making skills."

5
UP IN SMOKE

"Find a partner," said Mr. Alvarez.

Everyone scrambled.

Mari and Ashley chose each other, Ivan and I were in a group, and Kenrick and Max were partners.

"Kenrick, why didn't you want to be my partner?" I asked.

"No worries, Colter," said Kenrick.

"It's just that Max says he knows a lot about building fires."

"Oh yeah," said Ivan "Colter and I can out-fire you guys any day."

"You're on!" chuckled Kenrick.

"It's cool that we're partners. It'll be fun" said Max to Kenrick, "We'll build a neat fire!"

"You bet," laughed Kenrick.

Ranger Mendez explained the rules of the fire-starting competition.

"When I say go, your team may begin," said Ranger Mendez. "Build an A-frame base like I showed you earlier, from there, you are only allowed three matches to ignite your fire."

On either side of each group's fire ring were two sticks standing up from the ground with twine tied from the tip of one end to the other.

"If your team is successful at getting a flame, keep adding more wood until the fire begins to burn the twine. Whoever burns their twine in half first wins!"

"When I say 'go' our fire-starting challenge will begin," said Ms. Donner "one, two, three...go!"

Ivan and I sprang into action.

"How did he do that V-shape, Ivan?" I asked, while grabbing three larger sticks.

"Like this," Ivan said, matching the way Ranger Mendez had one stick resting on the other two. "Okay, now we need to put some little twigs on it."

I handed some twigs to Ivan, and he dumped them on top.

"Ivan, it won't catch like that," I said,

panicked, "Ranger Mendez said to do just a few at a time!"

"Nah, it'll work," Ivan said, lighting our first match.

He held the match under the twigs.

It went out!

Ivan lit a second match.

"Wait, Ivan. We need to clear out a few of these twigs," I said, clearing some out of the way. "This time hold your match a little longer and try to light a few different spots on the wood."

"Okay, I got this," said Ivan, lighting a few spots until the match caught the wood.

"Nice job, Ivan," I said. We watched the flame and waited. "Oh no! It went out again! I think we need to blow on it."

"Oh, no," Ivan said. "Some other groups have their fires lit!"

"Don't worry about them, let me try this time," I shouted.

"Sure thing," Ivan said, switching me places.

I laid down on my stomach in front of the twigs.

This was our last match.

We had to make it count.

I lit the match.

I placed the match under the twigs, watching the fire catch in a couple places.

I blew on the fire, helping it grow.

I accidently sucked in smoke and began to cough.

Taking my fedora hat off my head, I used it to help fan the flames.

"Oh no," Ivan said, "One group already burned through their twine!"

"Aw man," I said, fanning the flame. "It's okay. There are two spots left."

Ivan added more twigs to feed the fire. I kept fanning. Ivan added even more twigs.

The flames grew higher, inching toward the twine.

"Another team burned through their string, Ivan" I shouted.

"It's okay. Keep going," Ivan said. "We're almost there!"

Our fire began to singe the rope.

The twine caught fire!

It snapped!

"Third place," said Ranger Mendez, "Congratulations you guys!"

"Yes!" we shouted, high-fiving each other above the fire.

"We have our three winners," Ranger Mendez said, stopping the competition. "Ivan and Colter take third, Mari and Ashley come in second, and Max and Kenrick win first."

"We won!" shouted Kenrick to his partner Max.

"Hurray!" shouted Ashley. "We beat Ivan and Colter!"

"Whatever," grumbled Ivan. "You won't win next time, Ashley!"

6
RACE PARTNERS

Later that evening we gathered around the campfire, stuffing our faces with gooey s'mores.

"It's time to reveal the challenge we've been hinting at," Ms. Donner said. "We're having a race!"

Excited shouts and giddy whispers echoed through the campsite.

"We will be visiting a few parts of the park.

There may be clues left for teams to find to help you in the competition. Keep your eyes peeled.

Friday will be race day. The race is a 2.8-mile hike along the Lighthouse trail. The Lighthouse is a giant stone pillar at the end of the trail.

The first group to have both partners touch the base of the lighthouse will be the winners," said Ms. Donner.

"Does anyone have any questions about the race?" asked Mr. Alvarez, shading his eyes from the evening sunset.

"Can we ride bikes or ATVs?" Kenrick asked.

"No, this is a foot race," said Mr. Alvarez.

"Your partner from our fire-starting competition will be your race partner as well," said Ms. Donner.

"Wait, what?" asked Ivan.

"Your fire-starting partner is also your race partner," repeated Ms. Donner.

"So I can't be partners with Kenrick in the race, now?" I asked.

"Was he your fire-starting partner?" asked Ms. Donner.

"No," I said.

"Then it looks like you and Ivan are still partners," said Ms. Donner.

"Oh, great," Ivan said, grinning at me. "We're still stuck together."

"I know," I grinned back.

"But Ms. Donner," Kenrick said.

"Colter and I are best friends. I was partnered with Max for the fire-starting because he was a good fire-maker."

Max frowned.

"Then I'm sure the two of you will have fun running together too," smiled Ms. Donner.

"That's true," said Kenrick. "Max, I guess you're pretty awesome. I bet we're going to have lots of fun racing together."

"Thanks, Kenrick," smiled Max. "Let's show Ivan and Colter how races are run."

"Be warned" I said. "Ivan and I are going to leave you guys in the dust."

"Yeah, right", Max said.

Soon it was time for dinner.

"What do you think we're having for supper, Ivan?" I asked.

"How would I know, Colter?" Ivan replied, clutching his grumbling stomach.

"It smells tasty enough for me," said Mari, balancing on a rock.

Ashley laughed while kicking up dirt with her boots, "I bet ya a dollar it's beans and cornbread. We're in cowboy country after all."

"Pizza," Kenrick laughed.

"How would they get pizza all the way out here?" said Max. "Don't you know Palo Duro Canyon is fifty thousand miles from the nearest town? That's a twenty-day hike to pizza. No pizza could possibly stay warm for that many miles."

"So not pizza," I said, snickering at Max.

"Okay kids, time for brisket, beans, and cornbread," said Ranger Mendez.

45

"Yeehaw!" yelled Mari and me as we threw our hats in the air.

We grabbed our supper and found a spot around the campfire.

The sun began to set. It was dark now, and the evening breeze was brisk.

Everyone chatted around the campfire.

Half an hour later we were fed and full,

having scarfed down the brisket, sucked down the beans, and mopped up all the juices with the cornbread.

"Oh my!" exclaimed Interpretive Ranger Stacey. "I smell a night spider!"

"You smell a what?"

7
I SMELL A SPIDER

"What's a night spider?" asked Max "I've never heard of that type of spider before."

"Oh, just a spider you find at night," smiled Ranger Stacey.

"How do you smell a night spider?" Kenrick asked.

"You can't smell a spider," said Ivan. "That's ridiculous."

"Easy," said Ranger Stacey, sniffing the air. "Follow me and I'll show you".

Ivan, Mari, Ashley, Kenrick, Max, and I followed Ranger Stacey.

"It's easy to smell a spider at night," said Ranger Stacey. "All you have to do is sniff a lot. See." Ranger Stacey sniffed the air with her nostrils like a cartoon character does while trying to smell out a pie cooling on a window-seal.

Everyone sniffed the air loudly. Mmmmhhhhhhffffff.

"I smell one now!" laughed Ranger Stacey. With her flashlight leading the way, Ranger Stacey walked straight up to a spider sitting in the grass.

"Wow, that's awesome!" I said.

"What a cool critter," laughed Ashley.

"I bet it has terrific balance on all those legs," said Mari.

"But how do you know if you smell it?" asked Max. "This can't be real. I've seen lots of spiders- Brown Recluse, Charlie Horse, Black Widows, Daddy Longlegs- but I've never smelt a spider."

"You're right, silly," grinned Interpretive Ranger Stacey "you can't actually smell a spider, but do you want to learn how to trick others into thinking you can?"

"Sure," said Ivan with an evil grin. "I'd love to prank my parents."

"Turn on your flashlight with the light pointing out in front of you," began Ranger Stacey. "Now, bring the flashlight to eye level, so the light is shining right about where your eyes are also looking.

Most spiders have eight eyes. When you shine a light at a spider, those little eyes reflect the light back towards you. When you see a tiny little reflection, you have found the spider's eyes.

So, everyone, see if you can smell a spider!"

"Lame. That doesn't sound fun," said Ivan.

"Are you scared, Ivan?" I laughed.

"Um... No...," he stammered.

We turned on our flashlights and started looking around for spiders.

"I found one!" Kenrick screamed with excitement.

"Okay, let's go make sure!" said Ranger Stacey.

We followed Kenrick as he walked up to where his light was shining at the thick, brush-filled base of a mesquite tree.

A spider sat, staring back at us with his eight eyes. He was sitting on top of a pile of leaves at the base of the tree.

He looked fuzzy and creepy with the light shining on him in the dark.

"Wow. Great job finding this one," said Ranger Stacey. "This is a wolf spider, everyone. Do you see how it's black and brown? Sometimes people mistake wolf spiders for tarantulas.

It's surprising to see him sit still like this. Most don't like to be around people. A wolf spider is poisonous, so stay at a safe distance."

She motioned for us to step back, and we hurried away.

"Great job. Let's look for more spiders."

For the next ten minutes we searched trees, brush, and blades of grass.

We found at least ten spiders!

"Did you know that you swallow at least fifteen spiders a night?" Max said.

"Ew. Gross," gagged Ashley.

"Good job, everyone," said Ranger Stacey. "It's time return to our tents for the night."

"Aww man," we grumbled. "Can we look for one more?"

"Maybe tomorrow night," said Ranger Stacey, "but we've got a big morning planned, so it's off to bed."

Minutes later we were at camp. Kenrick and I were about to hop in our tent when we heard Max and Ivan screaming.

Wwwwaaaahhhh!!!

"Oh no," cried Ivan!

"This is awful," cried Max!

8
HORMIGAS

They were in the dark, creeping and crawling.

When we turned our flashlights on, we knew the insects in a heartbeat.

"Hormigas!" cried Ivan "Ants!"

"They're everywhere," cried Max. "Why? How? Where did they come from?"

Mr. Alvarez came rushing over. "Is everyone okay? I heard screaming."

"Mr. Alvarez, the helotes are marching in!" laughed Kenrick.

"What?" asked Mr. Alvarez, looking confused.

"The helotes!" screamed Max.

"Hormigas!" corrected Ivan.

"The ants go marching one by one, hurrah, hurrah!" I sang.

"Colter, not the time for singing," said Mr. Alvarez with a warning glance.

"Look, your tent is on top of an ant bed," Kenrick pointed with a flashlight "and your tent door is open!"

"Oh, no," said Ivan, opening the flap to peer inside at his chocolate bar.

"You left an open chocolate bar in there?" asked Max, frustrated.

"Yeah, but you left the tent door unzipped," said Ivan.

"Whatever," said Max. "Where are we going to sleep tonight? We can't stay in there. There are ants all over our beds."

"I've got an idea," said Mr. Alvarez "we've got some extra sleeping bags on the bus, but it doesn't look like the ants have gotten in your clothes bags. Grab your clothes, and each of you will sleep in another group's tent for tonight.

Ivan and Max nodded.

"Max, you can stay with Ben and Michael," continued Mr. Alvarez, "and Ivan, you can be in Kenrick and Colter's tent tonight."

"Yes sir," we said.

"Well guys," yawned Mr. Alvarez, "let's get to sleep."

Ivan, Kenrick, and I rushed to our tent, each trying not to be the one who got stuck in the middle.

"Scoot over," Kenrick grumbled, elbowing me in the side.

"Ouch, Kenrick, you're on my face," complained Ivan, smacking him with a pillow.

Our feet faced the tent entrance with Kenrick in the middle and Ivan and me on the sides.

Ivan and I were exhausted and began drifting to sleep, but Kenrick was wide awake.

"It's a bummer your tent had ants in it, Ivan."

"What do you call the world's largest ant, Colter?"

"I don't..." I began, but Kenrick cut in.

"A gi-Ant! Get it?"

"Zzzzzzzzzz," Ivan snored, fast asleep.

"Wow, Ivan falls asleep fast," Kenrick said. "Have you ever seen that superhero movie about that guy who became an ant? I heard it was pretty good. If I were a superhero, I'd want super speed, or super hearing, or the ability to control lightning."

"Good night, Kenrick," I chuckled, trying to go to bed.

"Goodnight, Colter," Kenrick laughed.

As I was falling asleep, I could still hear Kenrick cracking jokes. I drifted off, dreaming of the Lighthouse Race.

9
ANOTHER NOISE IN THE NIGHT

"What was that?" Ivan said, waking me up.

"What was what?" Kenrick yawned, half-asleep.

"I don't know," sneered Ivan. "That's why I asked."

"How would we know what it was?" I yawned. I stretched and scratched my head. "It's like 3 a.m. Let's go back to bed."

"Well, there's many possible suspects that there could be...out here at a state park," mumbled Kenrick, "but first you have to consider...what a group of pandas...would be doing...eating cereal...zzzzzzzzz."

Outside our tent, we heard something rustling the leaves. Something big.

"Kenrick, wake up," I said, nudging him awake again "don't you hear that sound?"

"I'm up, I'm up," Kenrick mumbled.

"What do you think it is, Colter?" Ivan asked. "Could it be a bison?"

"Probably," I said with a grin on my face, remembering our last camping trip. "We should definitely go check it out."

"Yyeaaahhh," whispered Ivan with sarcasm in his voice, "because that worked out real well last time."

"Remember gang...," stammered Kenrick "we're more afraid of celery... than ketchup is of us...zzzzzzzzzzz".

"Let's go check it out," I said, grabbing my fedora and placing it firmly on my head "grab your flashlights."

"Oh geez, not again," said Ivan, reaching across me to smack Kenrick awake "Hey, wake up, Kenrick. If I'm going, you're going."

"I'm up," yawned Kenrick.

We headed out into the early morning air.

The canyon was alive with noises, but we listened for a certain sound. We walked toward the sound of rustling, crunching leaves.

A twig snapped behind us!

"Hey, what are you three doing out of your tent this late at night?" asked Mr. Alvarez, shining his flashlight at us. "It's nearly 3 a.m."

"We could ask you the same question," said Ivan. "What are you doing up so late?"

"Ivan, don't play games with me, sir," said Mr. Alvarez. "I could send you on a bus back to school faster than you could say 'chicken nugget'.

"Yes sir," Ivan said, whispering slyly "... chicken nugget..."

"We were trying to find out what that rustling sound is, Mr. Alvarez," I said, pointing in the direction of the noise.

"Oh," said Mr. Alvarez, smiling. "I thought y'all were thinking about playing a prank on someone. Sure, let's go have a look."

"What?" Kenrick said, "You're going to let us go look?"

"Yeah. Why not?" Mr. Alvarez led our way in the dark through a giant patch of big bluestem grass. We were ten feet from the creature.

"Oh man, that smells funky," whispered Kenrick.

"Sorry," I said.

"I don't think it was you, Colter," Kenrick smirked.

"Hey Ivan," smiled Kenrick, "I've got a riddle of you."

"What is it, Kenrick?" asked Ivan.

"What's black and white and stinky all over?" said Kenrick, pointing.

Staring back at us in the moonlight was a skunk. He was fuzzy and playful-looking, but his teeth were small, sharp, and pointy. His tail was standing up.

"Well, it sees us, but it hasn't sprayed us yet," said Mr. Alvarez "we better back away before it does. It's probably trying to warn us."

"Can't we pet it?" I joked, making a move towards the skunk.

The skunk lunged toward me.

Ivan and I jumped back about ten feet to avoid the skunk.

"That skunk says 'stay back'," laughed Kenrick. We started backing away from the skunk. "You better listen to that skunk before you get sprayed and have to take a tomato juice bath." said Mr. Alvarez.

"He's not as cool as that cartoon skunk," Kenrick joked. We scooted out of the brush, back to our campsite.

10
ROCK GARDEN

The next morning Kenrick, Ivan, and I slept late. The sun had risen, peaking through the fabric of the tent.

Breakfast was called.

"Time to get up, guys," said Mr. Alvarez from outside the tent. "Adventure waits for no one. You'd better get some breakfast in your bellies before today's outings."

We slowly rolled out of the tent and hopped in line for breakfast. We were joined in line by Max, Ashley, and Mari.

"Morning sleepy heads," smiled Mari.

"Did you get your beauty rest?" joked Ashley.

"We had a pretty crazy night," I said.

"What? Was the smell of your filthy boy tent too much for you?" laughed Ashley.

"We chased down a skunk in the middle of the night," confessed Ivan, stretching.

"Yeah right," laughed Mari. "That's not true. You didn't see a skunk."

"It's true," Kenrick chimed in, smelling his shirt. "Believe me, it's true."

"Gross" gasped Ashley.

"Sure, sure," Mari said, rolling her eyes.

"Oh, nice! Breakfast tacos!" said Max as we reached the front of the line.

We grabbed some tortillas and loaded it with eggs, shredded cheese, bacon or sausage, and salsa.

We scarfed down our tacos as we sat by the last glowing embers of the morning campfire.

"Whoever is wanting to explore the Rock Garden, load up with me on the buses," bellowed Mr. Alvarez over the megaphone.

Interpretive Ranger Stacey was waiting to greet us at the Rock Garden.

Behind her were giant mounds of grey boulders jutting out in every direction, like chocolate chips on the surface of a cookie.

"Hello everyone, we're going to be exploring a small part of the Rock Garden Trail today," began Ranger Stacey, "so please remember to respect the plants and animals, be aware of your surroundings while staying on the trails, stay with a buddy or two, and drink plenty of water."

"Let's go on a walk," smiled Ranger Stacey, motioning for us to follow.

"These boulders are Trujillo sandstone.

They have been eroded over time by water and wind to create the unique shapes you see before you."

We were surrounded by boulders way taller than us on all sides as we kept walking.

"Many people have admired the wonderful features of Palo Duro Canyon. It's the second largest canyon in the U.S. next to the Grand Canyon," Ranger Stacey continued as we hiked, weaving through giant rocks.

"I would guess a few of you have heard of an artist named Georgia O'Keeffe. When she lived in this area, she said this place was 'a burning, seething cauldron, filled with dramatic light and color'.

Does anyone know what a cauldron is?" asked Ranger Stacey.

"I do!" shouted Max. "It's a giant pot cartoon characters use to make potions and stuff. They stir in it with a big wooden spoon."

Ranger Stacey laughed. "You're correct. It's a big, metal pot that is used to cook over a fire. Georgia O'Keeffe basically said that this place was a big pot overflowing with lots of beautiful colors."

"Do you see the colors everywhere around us?" asked Ranger Stacey. "What colors do you see?"

"Green!"

"Orange!"

"Yellow!"

"Maroon!"

"Black!"

"Yeah, good job everybody," laughed Ranger Stacey.

"Well," said Interpretive Ranger Stacey, stopping, "this will be our resting point. Everyone take a breather for five minutes, drink some water too, but don't wander off."

"Get with your racing partner. You are more than welcome to walk around within eyesight.

In fact, there is a volunteer up here who has a clue to give you for tomorrow's race. He will only give it to you if you can interpret his riddle. Good luck."

11
MEETING WITH A BEAR-MAN

"You go talk to him," Ivan said, nudging me.

"No way! You go talk to him," I said.

Twenty yards in front of us sat a grizzly bear. Or a man. Maybe both. He was a giant. He was a mountain. We were scared to go over.

"If anyone has a clue for the competition, it's definitely going to be him, Colter."

"Yeah, but he could eat us," I stammered.

The bear-man must have been seven-foot-tall and weighed at least 200 pounds. He wore an old fishing-style hat over his head, and half his clothes looked leather and hand-made. He wore Indian moccasins without socks.

His eyes were closed as he leaned back, resting against a rock.

His hands held a staff in front of him carved with unique symbols.

On his badge was written 'Texas State Park - Volunteer.' Under that, his name read 'Henry Randall'.

"He's asleep too," I said. "Maybe we should let him stay that way."

"Are you boys going to stand there all day," asked the sleeping bear-man, smirking and opening his eyes, "or are you going to come over and chit-chat?"

"Sor...sorry, sir, we thought you were asleep," stammered Ivan as we walked over.

"Oh, I never sleep," chuckled the bear-man with a laugh like Santa Claus, "and please, don't call me 'sir.' My name is Henry."

"Hi, Henry," I said, "my name's Colter and this is Ivan."

"Good to meet you," said Henry, shaking our hands, "I would guess you men are looking for some kind of clue for a race tomorrow?"

"Yes sir...I mean...Henry," said Ivan. "Do you have a clue for us?"

"I sure do," grinned Henry, slapping his knees, "but would you like to hear a little story first?"

"I'm not sure," I stammered. "We should probably be heading back to the rest of our group."

"It'll be a quick one," cut in Henry, beginning his story. "You'll both enjoy it. I promise."

"After I graduated high school, I decided to go live in the woods," said Henry.

"You what?" said Ivan, surprised.

"Now, hold on. I'm just getting started here," giggled Henry. "I walked into the Colorado wilds, and I decided I would try to survive out there alone."

"Did you see any animals?" I asked, shocked.

"I did. Big ones," said Henry, gesturing with his hands. "I saw moose, elk, and mountain lions. Lions, and tigers, and bears. Oh my!"

"While I was living in the woods, I discovered there are a few basic things you need to survive. If you have these three things, you've got a better shot of staying alive in the wilderness."

"What three things do you think are most important for survival?" Henry asked, leaning forward in his chair, braced against his walking stick.

"T.V.?" asked Ivan, giving a thumbs up.

"Food!" I suggested.

"Food! Good job!" laughed Henry. "When I lived in the woods there were two more things I also needed to survive. I needed a shelter to be under, and I needed water to drink."

"What did you make your shelter out of?" Ivan asked, curiously.

"Twigs and mud and string and such," chuckled Henry. "Well, you boys better head on back and join your group. I hear your leader calling."

"But Henry," I stammered, turning around to look at our group, "what about our clue, sir?"

But when we turned back to face Henry, he had vanished.

"What? He disappeared! How did he do that?" shouted Ivan, startled.

"Oh, don't worry about the clue, fellows," said a hidden voice, roaring with laughter. "I already gave it to you. You're smart young men. You'll figure it out."

12
FIRST CLUE

"What do you think Henry's clue was?" I asked Ivan "and how did he disappear like that?"

"I don't know, but too bad he couldn't have just told us the clue straight out before he disappeared," said Ivan. "That clue could make a huge difference in tomorrow's race."

"Well, what did he talk to us about? There must have been a clue in his story," I said.

"I don't know," sneered Ivan, kicking at the dirt. "He just said a bunch of stuff about living in the woods."

"Yeah, you're right," I said, confused. "He talked about animals, and he talked about what stuff you need to survive in the woods."

"That's it!" shouted Ivan. "I know what the first clue is!"

"Be quiet," I whispered, covering Ivan's mouth. "Everyone will hear us. We don't want to give away our clue."

"Eww, gross, Colter," Ivan spat. "Get your nasty hands off of my mouth."

A few teams were looking over at us including Mari, Ashley, Max, and Kenrick.

They were probably wondering why Ivan was yelling. I tried to throw them off our trail. "Oh, nothing," I said, looking over at them. "No clues over here."

"Okay everyone, time to hop on the bus," said Mr. Alvarez on the megaphone. "We're heading to 'Judy's Arch'."

We hiked back down the trail and jumped onto the bus. We sat in the back discussing our clues, hoping no one would hear us.

"Like I was saying," Ivan whispered, crouching close to me, "I know what the clue is."

"Well, what is it?" I whispered back.

"The three things you need to survive," Ivan counted on his fingers, "are food, water, and...Oh no. I can't remember the last one."

"Wasn't it a place to stay?" I asked.

"Yeah, that's it!" Ivan screamed.

"Shhh!" I said, checking around the bus to make sure no one had heard, then looking back at Ivan. "Awesome! I think you're right! I think we have the first clue!"

Interpretive Ranger Stacey was waiting to greet us when we pulled up in the bus.

"Hello everyone, we're going to be hiking up to 'Judy's Arch' this afternoon."

Ranger Stacey led the way as we followed a red dirt trail. The sun was high, but the clouds were overcast and a little dark.

The wind picked up. The blowing sand began to sting our arms and legs.

Ranger Stacey showed us plants along the hike. "These are called 'prickly pear cactus.' You can tell because of the Ping-Pong paddle looking parts of them. Be careful. They can stick you with their needles if you touch them.

The trail weaved back and forth, going past little, dried out streams and more patches of cactus. As the trail got a little rockier, I looked and noticed a hole way above in the canyon wall.

"What's that?" I asked Ranger Stacey, pointing towards the hole.

"That's Judy's Arch. That's where we're headed."

"All the way up there?" Kenrick asked.

"Yes sir," Ranger Stacey smiled. "It's not nearly as far as it looks."

"I don't think we'll be able to make it all the way up there by nightfall," Max predicted.

"Then we better get started," said Ranger Stacey, leading the way.

13
JUDY'S ARCH

We reached the base of the trail leading up to Judy's Arch. There were large, smooth rocks to scramble over on our way up to the cave.

"Watch your footing as we go up," said Ranger Stacey. "Each step is important because you never know if a boulder will be loose. Help each other over the rocks."

I noticed the walls on each side were red and crumbly.

"This is taking forever," moaned Ivan, breathing heavily.

"We're halfway there," smiled Interpretive Ranger Stacey, helping him over a rock.

"Our elevation must be at least 13,000 feet by now," calculated Max.

"No, this is just a little hike," smiled Mari, trekking on.

Ashley and Kenrick had fun scurrying from one large rock to another, pretending that the trail was lava.

The path grew smaller and rockier as we climbed up towards the mouth of Judy's Arch, closer to the cave.

I rested on a big mound of red dirt and looked back down the trail.

"Wow, I didn't realize how high we were getting," I said, whipping the red dirt from my forehead. "I don't think your sister will like the rest of this hike very much, Ivan."

"No, I don't think she will," said Ivan with a smirk. "She had a pretty rough time climbing at Caprock."

The entrance of Judy's Arch stood tall like pillars of a great museum. It must have been eighty feet high. The opening to the cave was extremely tall but narrow, with only enough room for two people to enter the cave at a time.

Running through the red rock inside the cave was a two-foot tall section of white rock. As soon as we entered the cave, we noticed the temperature inside was much cooler than it was outside.

Ranger Stacey spoke to our cave-packed class. "Take a little time to explore the cave. Be sure to look around. Friendly faces with volunteer badges might have clues for you for tomorrow's race."

"Echo, echo" Kenrick shouted, listening as the cave walls spoke back to him. "It's so neat in here. It's so neat in here."

"Wow, look way up there," laughed Mari, pointing up to the ceiling of the cave. "There's a hole with light coming through."

Way up at the top of the narrow, tall cave, light was streaming through a small opening.

We enjoyed exploring the inside of the cave for the afternoon.

Ranger Stacey's voice echoed. "Time for us to get ready for supper. I hope everyone found the second clue."

"Oh, no!" I whispered to Ivan. "We forgot to look for the second clue!"

"What? Oh no! What do we do?" whispered Ivan desperately.

"I don't know," I said. "Let's just hope no one else found the second clue either."

"Hey Ashley," Ivan said. "Did you and Mari find the clue in the cave?"

"W...well...of...of course found the clue..." said Ashley nervously. "Did y'all?"

"Yea...yeah..." I stammered.

Once Ashley walked on, I turned to Ivan. "Oh, no! They have more clues than us!"

14
RACE DAY

It was finally race day!

There was a buzz of excitement in the air as partners gathered together over breakfast to strategize how they would be victorious.

I overheard someone say that they had competed in marathons before and so this race would be easy.

Another group decided that, to save energy, they would give their partner a piggy-back ride for a while then switch. One girl thought about running the race bare-foot, saying she would run faster without the extra weight of her tennis shoes.

Mr. Alvarez tried to get our attention, but everyone was too excited. As a last resort, he pulled out the megaphone. "Hey everyone, let's listen to Ranger Mendez so we can get this race started!"

"Thank you, Mr. Alvarez," said Ranger Mendez. "After breakfast we'll make our way to the Lighthouse trailhead where our race will begin," continued Ranger Mendez. "It's a 2.8-mile hike to the Lighthouse."

"Hurray!" everyone shouted.

"The first group to have both partners touch the base of the lighthouse will be the winners of our competition.

You'll use your clues at two different stations located at the mile one and mile two marker of the race.

There will be adults stationed at different checkpoints a quarter-mile apart to make sure you don't get lost and stay on course.

Any questions so far?" asked Ranger Mendez.

"Nmo sur" we mumbled, shaking our heads with breakfast tacos tucked in our cheeks.

"Alright, good," continued Ranger Mendez. "Also, the winners of our previous fire-starting competition will receive a one-minute head start."

I leaned over towards Ivan quietly as Ranger Mendez continued giving instructions. "We've got no shot at winning without that second clue since Ashley and Mari have both clues."

"Did Max and Kenrick get any of the clues?" asked Ivan.

"I don't know," I confessed.

"It's okay. We'll be fine," said Ivan. "I've got a plan."

"Oh good! What is it?" I said sarcastically.

"We'll get a quick start, and get a good way in front of everyone else. We're fast runners," Ivan said, "so when we get to the part where we don't have the clue, we can take more time and see how other teams do it."

"Sounds like an okay plan to me," I shrugged, "except, oh wait, Kenrick and Max are fast runners and have a head start with us too like Mari and Ashley do."

"You're totally right," said Ivan. "There's no way we'll win."

"Ready for the race, guys?" Max whispered.

"Oh yeah," said Ivan. "We've got this in the bag."

"How are y'all feeling about the race, Kenrick?" I asked.

"Feeling good. It'll be fun," Kenrick replied.

"Ready to lose, losers?" whispered Mari and Ashley.

"Yeah right," grumbled Ivan. "You'll see."

"Oh, we'll see, will we?" sneered Ashley.

"Yeah!" I said confidently.

"Yeah?" said Mari.

After Ranger Mendez finished giving instructions, we headed for the bus.

"Stay on the trail. Drink lots of water. Stay together," said Ranger Stacey at the Lighthouse trailhead.

"Accidents can happen out here. Each checkpoint has volunteers equipped with first aid kits," added Ranger Mendez. "Be safe and have fun. Teams to the starting line."

"On your mark. Get set. Go!"

15
ON THE RUN

"Hurry up, Colter," Ivan shouted.

"I'm coming," I yelled back, pushing my legs to move quicker. My shoes dug into the rough dirt path, kicking up dust as I went.

We ran along the trail in the cool morning air. The sun was just rising over the canyon wall.

The light turned the trees and cactus from a sleepy blue to a lively green.

"We're in the lead," I screamed, smiling.

"It's a miracle," laughed Ivan, in front of me, "let's keep up the pace and don't look back."

Pretty close on our tails were Ashley and Mari.

"Where are Kenrick and Max?" I shouted to Ivan.

"I don't know, but keep going," he shouted back.

Ahead, I saw the painted walls that formed the caprock. In the base of the canyon were dry river beds and wild flowers. A yellow lizard darted across the trail, scurrying to find shelter from predators.

Everything ahead of us was silent except for the sound of chirping crickets and tweeting birds.

I ran with my canteen attached to my hip, making a sloshing sound as I went.

We could hear the sound of stampeding feet hitting the hard ground. The feet were hoping to catch up and pass us to take the lead.

A large gust of wind slammed into us, trying to knock us over. We kept pushing harder.

The wind spat dirt at our skin, the grains of sand stinging us like little mosquitoes trying to suck our blood.

We'd squint our eyes, hoping to avoid getting dirt in them. I also shielded my eyes with the brim of my fedora.

We shut our mouths tight, hoping not to eat sand for a second breakfast.

"Let's hope this high wind slowed everyone else down too," Ivan said, spitting dirt from his mouth as he ran faster.

"It didn't slow Ashley and Mari down much, Ivan," I yelled, looking back to see them close behind. "They're still gaining on us."

"We're coming for you guys," yelled Ashley, running fast with a wild look in her eyes.

Ahead on the trail, the path cut into two directions.

People were standing at the intersection: bicyclists, a young married couple, and a lady trying to get good cell phone reception.

"Oh no," I shouted. "Ivan, look up ahead. The path goes in two directions. Which way do we go?"

"I'm not sure," Ivan yelled back, "but we need to decide fast or they'll catch us."

"Those bikers are blocking the trail on the right," I puffed, catching my breath. "I bet it's a trail that dead-ends, like a few we found earlier."

"I bet you're right," said Ivan, breathing deeply, "so that means the left trail is the one we should take!"

"Right," I yelled.

"Right?" he shouted back.

"No, left!" I replied.

"Okay, no left, so we'll go right, right?" he shouted, confused.

"No. Left is right!" I yelled louder.

"Well, if we're not going right then left is all that's left, right?" Ivan asked.

"What? Right. Yeah, take a left," I screamed as we neared the turn.

"Okay, I'm taking a left," pointed Ivan.

We went left at the fork in the trail. It began taking us around the side of the canyon wall.

"They're still following us, Ivan," I said, looking back to see Ashley and Mari, "and they're catching up!"

"Keep going! Don't look back!" shouted Ivan.

16
NECK AND NECK

"How do they run so fast?" I shouted to Ivan "and where are Max and Kenrick?"

"How do who run so fast?" laughed Mari, as she ran just a little behind me.

"There is no way you guys will beat us," said Ashley, running right next to me.

We sped along the path, our teams neck and neck, breathing hard. Sweat started beading on our foreheads as the sun rose higher in the sky.

The trail was narrowing, dotted along the side with prickly bushes and pokey cactus plants.

It was dry and hot.

A tumbleweed crossed our path. Ivan kicked it out of the way as he ran.

"Ivan, we can't run like this forever," I said, gasping for air, "We're going to have to stop at some point to drink some water."

"No way, Colter," he shot back, "if we do that, they'll pass us."

"Colter's probably got a good point, Ashley," stammered Mari. "We'll wear ourselves out too fast if we don't stop for a quick water break."

"Yeah, guys," I chimed in. "The ranger said if we aren't careful, it's easy to get dehydrated out here."

"Well, I'll only stop if Ivan will stop," Ashley said, taking a deep breath as she continued to run.

"No way," Ivan screamed, quickening his pace. "It's a trick."

"They're not trying to trick us, Ivan," I said. "We'll stop together, and after a quick drink, we'll keep going."

"Yeah," said Mari, "the other groups aren't even close to catching up with us. We can't even see them back there."

"Okay, okay," Ivan agreed. "We'll stop up there in the shade of that bush, but not too long because Kenrick is fast and could catch up to us."

As we reached the shade, we sat down in the dirt, relaxing our throbbing feet for a moment. We chugged our water and tried to catch our breaths. Ivan drank with water running down the front of his shirt.

"I'm thirsty as a camel," said Mari.

"Camels aren't thirsty," I said. "They have humps to store water."

"Sally the camel has five humps," laughed Ashley.

"Who?" I said.

"Now, Ashley!" yelled Mari.

Ashley and Mari jumped to their feet and took off. Just like that, they were on the trail again, running hard, taking the lead.

Ivan and I scrambled to our feet, in hot pursuit.

"Hey, that's not fair," I yelled ahead to them. "You didn't say go!"

"No one ever said we had to say go," laughed Ashley, looking back at Ivan and me.

Ivan was angry. I could see it on his face. We ran quickly, determined to catch up.

We followed the winding trail under the blistering sun.

We ran and ran for a long time until we had to stop again in the shade for another break.

"You won't pull a fast one on us again," said Ivan, glaring at Ashley.

"Sure, we won't," smirked Ashley.

Mari stuck her tongue out.

"Hey," said Mari, "where is everybody?"

"What do you mean?" Ivan asked.

"Well, we've been stopped for a while," Mari explained. "Shouldn't a group have at least caught up to us by now?"

"No way," laughed Ivan. "We're way too fast."

"Wait, Ivan, Mari may have a point," I said. "Where is everybody? Where is Kenrick and Max?"

"Shouldn't we have at least seen a checkpoint by now?" Mari said.

"Yeah," I answered.

"Do you think we could have taken a wrong turn?" Ashley asked. "Which way is the way back?"

"No. We went the right way. I'm sure of it," Ivan said shortly. "And the way back is that way."

"No, Ivan," I said, pointing the opposite direction. "The way back is this way."

"Um, guys," Mari said. "I think we're lost."

17
WHAT TO DO?

"This is your fault," Ivan shouted, pointing at Ashley.

"Hey!" shouted Ashley, getting in Ivan's face, "how is this my fault?"

"If you wouldn't have tricked us when we stopped, none of this would have happened," Ivan said.

"Are you kidding me?" Ashley screamed, clenching her fists. "That's the silliest thing I've ever heard of!"

"No, it's not," Ivan continued. "It makes perfect sense!"

"Your face doesn't make perfect sense," laughed Mari nervously at her brother while balancing on a rock.

"Yeah, and actually, it's all your fault" shot back Ashley. "We were following y'all most of the time. So you're the ones who got us lost."

"That's crazy!" shouted Ivan. "And Mari, what are you doing balancing on that stupid rock?"

"Be quiet!" yelled Mari, still keeping her balance. "I'm trying to concentrate and figure out what to do next."

"Oh, you just be quiet," said Ivan to Mari.

"Hey!" Ashley stared at Ivan, raising a tight fist, "nobody tells my friend to be quiet."

"I can if I want to," huffed Ivan. "Mari's my little sister. She has to do what I say."

"EVERYBODY BE QUIET!" I yelled.

Everyone stopped and stared at me.

"Listen, we're lost. It doesn't matter how we got lost, but we're lost," I stammered. "Mari's right. We need to figure out what to do next."

"HELP! HELP! HELP!" yelled Ashley at the top of her lungs. "WE'RE LOST! HELP!"

Ivan shrugged, then started yelling too, "HHHHEEELLLLPPPP!!!!"

"HHHHEEELLLLPPPPP!!!!"

We yelled until we couldn't yell anymore.

"Well, what do we do now?" I said.

"I don't know," said Ivan, "but I'm sure there are monsters out here after dark."

"Stop trying to scare people, Ivan," said Ashley.

At that moment, a little, foot-long black snake with a red stripe around its neck slithered across the path in front of us.

"Aaaahhhhh!" yelled Ivan.

"Calm down," laughed Mari. "It's just a tiny Ring-necked snake."

"Hey, don't laugh at me," growled Ivan. "It's your fault we're in this mess in the first place."

"Oh, here we go again," Mari said, still balancing on the boulder.

"Get off of that stupid rock and fix this mess you got us into," said Ivan.

"What are we going to do, guys?" Ashley asked anxiously.

"I don't know," I said seriously.

"Aaahhhh!!!" Mari screamed.

I turned around just in time to glimpse Mari losing her balance on the rock. Frantically trying to get her footing, she slipped and fell face-first into a prickly pear cactus!

18
CLOSE ENCOUNTERS OF THE CACTUS KIND

"Get me out of here! Get me out of here! Help!" Mari sobbed at the top of her lungs. Her cries for help were a mess of tears and terror.

"What do we do? What do we do?" shouted Ashley, watching Mari helplessly pinned face-down in the cactus.

"I don't know. I don't know," Ivan panicked, pacing back and forth.

"Mari, focus. Where are the cactus needles sticking in you?" I said.

"I don't know," Mari wailed. "It hurts so much!"

"We're going to help you, Mari," sobbed Ashley, wrapping her arms around herself while tears streamed down her face.

"Mari, listen," I continued, bending closer to her. "I know it hurts, but if you can describe where you're stuck, we can get you out of there, okay?"

"O...okay," Mari whimpered.

She thought for a moment then answered. "The needles are mostly in my left arm and on my left side.

The right side of my stomach is leaning on a fallen branch, keeping me above the rest of the cactus."

"Okay, that's perfect," I said. "Do you think you can stand up out of there?"

"No, I don't." she continued to sob. "I can't stand up, and I can't roll over. I'd get stuck by more needles."

"Could we lift you out of there?" suggested Ivan, his face distraught.

"I, I think so," she cried.

"What if we pulled on the back of your shirt?" I said. "We can lift you out of there."

"I don't know," Mari stammered. "Please, just get me out of here!"

"Okay, let's pull her out!" shouted Ivan quickly, pushing his way closer to his sister.

"But Ivan, wait, we don't know if it'll work," said Ashley. "We could hurt her even more."

"It's our best bet, Ashley," Ivan whispered. "We have to help her."

"Just try!" cried Mari. "It hurts so bad. Please get me out of here!"

Ivan leaned over as close to his sister as possible, grabbing the back of her shirt.

"Okay,'" Ivan began, "I'm going to lift you out. I promise."

"Try to keep your legs straight so you don't get any needles in your knees as Ivan pulls you out," I said.

"Tell us when you're ready, Mari."

All was quiet for a second.

"I'm ready," she sniffled.

Ivan, Ashley, and I looked at each other, nodding our heads.

"Okay," said Ivan calmly, "one, two, three."

On the count of three, he slowly pulled Mari out. She screamed as he plucked her out of the cactus.

Ivan lifted her out of the cactus, out of the muck and needles. Ashley and I helped set her feet on solid ground, we and gave her a firm place to stand.

Now standing on her own two feet, Mari began trembling and shaking from shock.

"Get them out. Get them out," she jumped, her eyes wild.

Covering her left arm, dark needles and cactus pads stuck out from her skin.

Bright red blood formed in little circles at the base of each needle.

"Okay, hold still," I said. I reached over to pluck a cactus pad the size of a ping pong paddle out of Mari's arm.

She was moving too much. As I reached to pull the paddle, it freed from her skin and instead got stuck in my own hand.

"Ouch," I screamed, shaking the bright green cactus pad free from my hand. I watched as tiny streams of red covered the surface of my palm and a single drop dripped to the ground.

I quickly wiped the blood on to my pants and went back to help Mari.

"Please don't pull them anymore," Mari cried. "Please, someone go get help."

"I'm staying here with you, Mari," Ashley cried, gently brushing Mari's forehead.

"Ivan, you and Ashley are faster runners," I thought out loud. "Maybe you two could run down the trail to find help."

"I'm not leaving my sister, Colter" stammered Ivan.

"Ivan, listen," I pleaded. "You're the best bet of helping her the quickest. Go run and find help for your sister."

"Yeah Ivan, you and I can go different directions down the trail," said Ashley. "One of us might run into someone with a first aid kit who could help Mari."

"Okay, you two go. I'll stay here and take care of her," I said, reaching for two water bottles. "Be careful, and take these with you."

"Got it, Colter," nodded Ivan seriously, taking the water bottle. "We'll be back in a minute, Mari."

With that, Ashley and Ivan were running opposite ways down the trail, looking for help.

19
DON'T LEAVE ME

"Colter," Mari said, with tears in her eyes. "What if they can't find someone?"

"They'll find someone. They won't let you down. Ivan's your brother. He loves you," I said, trying to comfort her. "They'll find someone. They have to."

"Here, drink some water," I said, opening the water bottle.

"Thanks, Colter," she said, taking a long drink.

"Can you sit down with those cactus needles in you?"

"I think so," Mari sniffled, slowly taking a seat on a rock as we waited for help.

"Is there anything I can do?" I asked, knowing she was in a lot of pain.

"It just really hurts. Just don't leave me."

"I won't. I promise."

"Where are they? Why is it taking so long? Did they get lost?"

"No, I'm sure one of them has found help and is on their way back."

"Colter..." "Yeah," I replied. "What's up?"

"I'm sorry," she said, lowering her head.

"What?" I asked. "For what?"

"We lied yesterday to you and Ivan. We really only had one clue. We didn't find the other one at Judy's Arch."

I smiled, "Well, then I'm sorry too."

"Why's that?" she said, tilting her head.

"We only had one clue too," I chuckled.

Mari smirked. "So, neither of us had a great chance at winning this race?" She giggled, then winced at the painful needles.

"Are you okay?" I asked again.

"Yeah, I just have to remember not to move," Mari said. She paused and then spoke again. "I think you're a good friend, Colter. Thanks for staying with me."

"You're welcome, Mari," I said. "I'm really glad to be here with you."

"Colter, it really hurts."

"I'm sorry, Mari. Help is coming."

20
BRAVE

Suddenly, we heard shouting from down the trail.

"Help! We're over here!" we screamed.

Soon Ivan came running towards us.

"Ivan, what happened?" said Mari.

"I followed the trail for a little bit before it dead-ended.

I couldn't find anyone on the trail. I'm so sorry."

"It's okay, Ivan. I'm sure Ashley will find help."

"Wait, is she not back yet?" asked Ivan.

"Not yet," I said.

Mari winced in pain again. She was starting to look pale.

"I have to keep looking for help," Ivan said. "Who knows, maybe Ashley got lost on the trail."

"Ivan wait..." I started. "Do you hear that?"

"Hello? Is anyone out there?" A familiar voice rang through the air.

"We're over here!" we shouted.

Ashley, Ms. Donner, and Ranger Mendez came racing down the trail toward us.

"We see you," shouted Ashley.

Soon, they were running up to us.

"Are you guys okay?" asked Ms. Donner.

Ranger Mendez bent down next to Mari, asking about her wounds.

"It really hurts," she grimaced. "I have cactus needles in my left arm and in my left side."

Ranger Mendez began pulling out pliers from his multi-tool.

"What are those for?" panicked Mari.

"May I help you by pulling out these needles?" Ranger Mendez asked.

"Yes sir," Mari said, sniffling.

"It'll be okay," Ranger Mendez said. "It may hurt a bit, but we need to pull those needles out."

Mari whimpered.

"You're going to be okay," reassured Ashley.

As Ranger Mendez began pulling the cactus pads and needles from her skin, Mari began to cry again.

She was brave as needles were pulled. The cactus was still trying to cling to her skin.

Minutes later, Ranger Mendez had removed the rest of the cactus needles. He dressed

Mari's wounds with ointment and gauze from his first aid kit.

"How does that feel?" Ranger Mendez asked as he finished wrapping Mari's wounds.

"That feels a lot better," she said, still wincing at the pain.

"Mari, do you think you can walk?" Ranger Mendez asked.

"I can walk," she said, rising slowly to her feet.

"Let's get you out of here," smiled Ranger Mendez.

"Ranger Mendez, Colter got a few needles in his hand while trying to help me," Mari said. "Can you bandage him up too?"

Soon my hand was wrapped up as well. I didn't realize how bad just a few needles would hurt when they were being pulled out. I can't imagine how horrible the pain must have been for Mari.

We began walking back down the trail. Mari was tough. She wasn't slowed down much by her bandaged arm.

"Here is where your group took a wrong turn," said Ranger Mendez, walking over to a sign, pointing at its two directional arrows.

"You took a left and went on the Capitol Peak Trail," said Ranger Mendez. "The Lighthouse Trail goes to the right from here."

"Aww man," frowned Ivan. "Those bicyclers were blocking the sign earlier."

"That must be why we didn't see each other," said Ms. Donner. "I was helping the bicyclists with directions. I'm so sorry, kids."

"It's okay Ms. Donner.

"We better start hiking back towards the trailhead," she said.

"But," asked Mari, "what about finishing the race?"

"You can't finish the race with your arm like that, Mari," said Ms. Donner.

"I really can," Mari continued. "It doesn't hurt that bad anymore with the bandage on my arm."

"I don't know," replied Ms. Donner.

"Please," Mari pleaded. "We want to see what the Lighthouse looks like."

"Well, is everyone still okay with hiking to the Lighthouse?" asked Ms. Donner.

"Of course, we are," I said. "We know we didn't win, but we still want to see it!"

"Yeah," chimed in Ivan, "It would be cool to see the lighthouse."

"Can we please, Ms. Donner?"

21
THE LIGHTHOUSE

"Okay," smiled Ms. Donner. "We'll go to the Lighthouse, but we have to stay on the trail this time."

Nearing the Lighthouse, the landscape began to change. The trail grew steep and narrow. Before long, we could only walk in a single-file line.

"There it is, kids," pointed Ranger Mendez. "That's the Lighthouse."

"Where?" asked Ivan, pulling out his binoculars for a better look.

"Look way up there, through the trees," pointed Ranger Mendez again. "That's the Lighthouse."

"Wow," said Mari. "We've still got a long way to go."

"Are you sure your arm is okay for this?" asked Ms. Donner.

"I was born ready," she joked.

When we reached some shade under a tree, we took a break to catch our breath and drink some water.

I noticed the trail was taking a left, up a steep, rocky hill with lots of tree covering.

"This is the last push to the Lighthouse," said Ranger Mendez. "It gets pretty gnarly up there."

"What do you mean by gnarly?" asked Ivan.

"Challenging," Ranger Mendez replied. "The trail won't be flat. There will be crevices and washouts, big boulders and loose sand. We will have to navigate carefully."

"Cool," I smirked. "Let's do this."

We hiked up the trail. Our feet were planted as we stepped to keep from slipping. I climbed next to Mari. Ivan walked next to Ashley.

Mari did great, even with her bandaged arm. We helped each other climb by lending our good hand to help the other person balance, making sure our partner wouldn't fall.

We reached the final stretch of the hike to the Lighthouse. We stood on a steep, red hill of dirt and rocks.

We were only one hundred yards away.

Looking up, the Lighthouse rose up like a massive pillar. To see the whole thing, I had to crane my neck pretty high towards the sky.

The base of the Lighthouse was gigantic, slowly becoming smaller in size as it jutted straight up into the air. It was made up of mostly red rock, but there were waves of white rock that would ring around it in clever patterns.

There were shelves along the way, where rocks would push out from the side.

At the very top, the rock formation changed suddenly from red to white, making it look like the Lighthouse was shining a beacon of light at the tip-top.

We followed the trail as it cut to the left, then back around to the right. Finally, we crawled over a ledge and on to the base of the Lighthouse!

"We made it!"

Ashley, Mari, Ivan, and myself high-fived and celebrated with cool sips of water as Kenrick and Max approached.

"Hey, you guys," said Kenrick. "Wow, what happened to your arm, Mari?"

"Oh, it's fine," she smiled bravely.

"Guess what," said Kenrick. "Max and I won!"

"Congratulations!" I shouted.

"How did you guys win?" asked Ivan curiously.

"Do you remember the clues?" asked Kenrick. "Each clue was a part of a cool puzzle that you had to complete during the race to keep going."

"A puzzle?" I questioned. "Huh, I guess we got lost before we ever came across a clue puzzle."

"So, how'd you do on the puzzles?" asked Ashley.

"Kenrick and I got them finished quick by putting our heads together and solving them," said Max. "Then Kenrick helped push me to run hard in the last part of the race so we could win!"

"Yeah, we were a great team," said Kenrick.

"Wow," Mari said. "Congrats you guys!"

I was glad Kenrick won, but I was also feeling really sad that Ivan and I didn't win. I tried to cheer up by exploring the Lighthouse some more. I wish we could have done better. I wish we wouldn't have taken the wrong turn. We could've won.

I was gladder that we didn't stay lost. I was gladdest that Mari was okay.

I focused on what lay ahead of me. The base of the Lighthouse was flat, but there were drop offs on each side. The pillar stretched high, making anyone who stood next to it look like the tiniest little ant.

All around, stretched out into a 360-degree view, was Palo Duro Canyon.

Standing at the edge of the drop-off, I stopped to take a long look.

I saw mesquite trees clustered together. I listened to the sound of birds chirping. I felt the gentle breeze flow across my face.

I felt free.

Ivan and Kenrick came and stood beside me.

"Hey, Colter," Kenrick said. "You okay?"

"Yeah," I replied. "Just taking a look at the canyon."

"What a race," smiled Kenrick.

"Yeah," laughed Ivan. "I won't ever forget it. That's for sure."

Mari and Ashley soon came over to join us, looking out over the landscape.

"I'm glad you're okay, Mari," I said.

"Thanks, Colter," she replied. "I'm glad I had you guys and Ashley to help me."

"What a crazy adventure," laughed Ashley.

Ranger Mendez walked over to us. He pointed out into the canyon. "Do you see that Aoudad sheep herd way down there?"

"Oh yeah," said Mari. "Cool!"

"Look at their neat horns!" said Kenrick.

"Well," smiled Ranger Mendez, "I think they've got it figured out."

"What do you mean?" I asked, staring at the Aoudads.

"You see, they travel together," said Ranger Mendez.

"Yeah, so?" said Ivan, looking through his binoculars.

"That's a secret they know," smiled Ranger Mendez.

"What secret?" asked Ashley.

"Aoudads know that it doesn't matter how fast you get somewhere," spoke Ranger Mendez. "What matters is who's by your side."

I thought. I glanced over at my friends.

I smiled.

Thank you to my beautiful wife Jordan for teaching me that dreams can grow into reality if you're willing to fight for them.

Thank you to my illustrator, cover artist, and friend Shawn Taylor for your always outstanding artwork.

Special thanks to my first Palo Duro readers: Andrea H., MacKinze S., and Weston M.

Thank you to Laura W. and Lisa J. What wonderful stories I've heard of annual field trips to Palo Duro under your leadership.

Thank you to LTC, Texas Baptist Men, and the Royal Ambassadors for teaching me the joys of the outdoors.

Thank you to my family.

Lastly, thank you to all those who work hard to protect the natural beauty of our wonderful state of Texas.

Jefferson Marshall

is an author, teacher, and outdoor enthusiast living in Wolfforth, Texas.

Shawn Taylor

is an illustrator, painter, teacher, and worship leader living in Pampa, Texas.

Coming Soon:

#3
Texas State Park Adventures

at

Garner State Park

Find out more at:
texasstateparkadventures.com